S0-CFD-991

I dedicate this to my mom, who must have been a professional problem solver raising me as a kid!

What's the Problem?

A Story Teaching Problem Solving

Written by
Bryan Smith

Illustrated by
Lisa M. Griffin

BOYS TOWN
Press

Boys Town, Nebraska

What's the Problem?
Text and Illustrations Copyright © 2019 by Father Flanagan's Boys' Home
ISBN: 978-1-944882-38-9

Published by the Boys Town Press
13603 Flanagan Blvd.
Boys Town, NE 68010

All rights reserved under International and Pan-American Copyright Conventions. Unless otherwise noted, no part of this book may be reproduced, stored in a retrieval system, or transmitted in any form or by any means, electronic, mechanical, photocopying, recording or otherwise, without express written permission of the publisher, except for brief quotations or critical reviews.

For a Boys Town Press catalog, call **1-800-282-6657**
or visit our website: **BoysTownPress.org**

Library of Congress Publisher's Cataloging-in-Publication Data

Smith, Bryan (Bryan Kyle), 1978- author. | Griffin, Lisa M., 1972- illustrator.

What's the problem? : a story teaching problem solving

Boys Town, NE : Boys Town Press, [2019] | Series: Executive FUNction. | Audience: grades K-6. | Summary: This story introduces and encourages readers to use SODAS (Situation, Options, Disadvantages, Advantages, and Solution) as a way to logically and thoughtfully solve any problem, from the silly to the serious. This is the sixth book in the Executive FUNction series, which skillfully weaves skill teaching into humorous storylines.-- Publisher.

ISBN: 978-1-944882-38-9

LCSH: Problem solving in children--Juvenile fiction. | Stress management for children--Juvenile fiction. | Children--Time management--Juvenile fiction. | Self-confidence in children--Juvenile fiction. | Self-reliance in children--Juvenile fiction. | Children--Life skills guides--Juvenile fiction. | CYAC: Problem solving--Fiction. | Stress management--Fiction. | Time management--Fiction. | Self-confidence--Fiction. | Self-reliance--Fiction. | Conduct of life--Fiction. | BISAC: JUVENILE FICTION / Social Themes / Self-Esteem & Self-Reliance. | JUVENILE FICTION / Social Themes / Values & Virtues. | SELF-HELP / Self-Management / Stress Management. | SELF-HELP / Self-Management / Time Management. | JUVENILE NONFICTION / Social Topics / Self-Esteem & Self Reliance. | EDUCATION / Counseling / General.

LCC: PZ7.1.S597 W536 2019 | DDC: [Fic]--dc23

Printed in the United States
10 9 8 7 6 5 4 3 2 1

Boys Town Press is the publishing division of Boys Town, a national organization serving children and families.

Hey everyone!
It's me, Braden.

Do any of you have
whiny brothers or sisters who
always get their way?

It's so annoying.

3

My brother, Blake, and I argue **ALL THE TIME.** Our mom says we both need to become better problem solvers. I say Blake just needs to listen to me – *his smarter, older brother*. Then everything would be fine.

Things sure weren't okay two days ago when Blake and I walked into the game room and grabbed the video game controller at the same time.

The TUG of WAR was on!

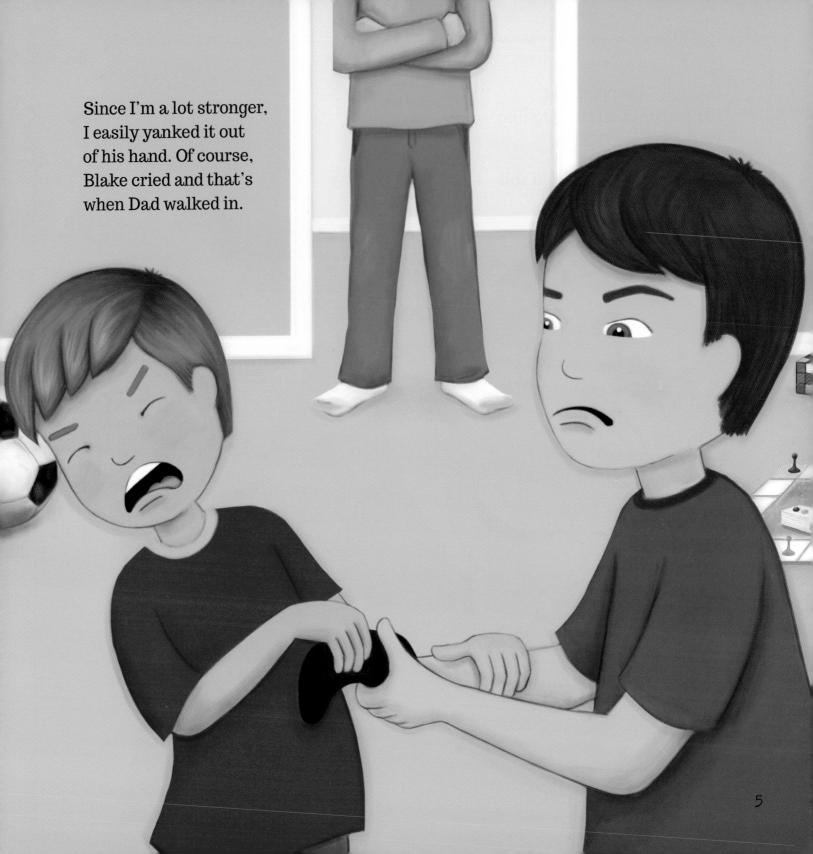

Since I'm a lot stronger, I easily yanked it out of his hand. Of course, Blake cried and that's when Dad walked in.

5

"Enough!" snapped Dad.
"I'm so sick of all this arguing.
You both need SODAS!"

Blake and I were excited and
jumped up and down.

Really!
I'll take
root beer!

Me too!

6

"Nice try, but I'm not talking about root beer. 'SODAS' is something your grandpa taught me when I was your age. SODAS helped me solve problems and make better choices," explained Dad.

"It works like this...

4 STEPS to Problem Solving (using SODAS)

1. Identify the problem **Situation**.
2. Think of all your **Options** for dealing with the situation.
3. Consider the possible **Disadvantages** and **Advantages** of each option.
4. Choose an option as your **Solution** and then do it."

"Why should we do ALL that?"
I wanted to know.

7

"For lots of reasons. It makes you think of options besides the first impulsive thing that pops into your head. Instead of making problems worse, you'll make better choices."

"Oh," I said. "I guess we can give it a try."

"Great. Let's start with **number one,** identifying the problem situation."

"That's easy. We both want to play the same video game, and it's a one-player game," I said.

> **1** <u>Problem/Situation</u>
>
> Play video game

"Correct. Now let's think of the **options** you have in this situation."

"Blake could take a nap
while I play," I suggested.

"Or, we could just sell YOU to
another family," shouted Blake.

2
<u>Options</u>

Blake takes a nap while I play.

Sell Braden to another family.

"Boys, when thinking about options, you need to think of things that are fair and doable. Why not a game of rock-paper-scissors to decide who gets to play first? Or better yet, why not play a game together?"

"There are no two-player games we want to play right now. Can I just lock Blake out of the game room?" I asked.

"You know that's not fair, Braden. Seriously, how about a game of rock-paper-scissors?"

Blake and I looked at each other, shrugged our shoulders and said, "Maybe."

Maybe

"Okay! Now let's **make a list of the disadvantages and advantages** of the options we talked about."

3

Disadvantages
Advantages

	DISADVANTAGES	ADVANTAGES
BLAKE TAKES A NAP	- Blake gets madder and instead of sleeping, he argues the whole time. - Mom and Dad get mad.	- Braden is happy and plays first. - The longer Blake sleeps, the longer Braden gets to play.
SELL BRADEN	- Against the law. - Mean. - Not doable.	- Blake gets everything!
ROCK-PAPER-SCISSORS	- You might lose.	- Fair way to decide who plays first. - Mom and Dad are happy.

4

Solution

"Now, you two need to choose a solution."

We both agreed rock-paper-scissors was our best option. **Blake won - UGH!**

But it didn't take long before I had my turn, so I guess it wasn't **SO** bad. Maybe I could try this problem-solving thing again.

The next day in art class, my friend Savannah was **MAD.**
Friends told her Mary had called her a **MEANIE.**

"I'll get her back," Savannah declared. "I'm going to tell
everyone Mary's hair looks like a rat's nest!"

"I'm not talking about something you drink, silly. The **SODAS** I'm talking about help you solve problems, like the one you have with Mary. Here's how it works."

4 STEPS to Problem Solving

1. Identify the problem **S**ituation.

2. Consider the **O**ptions for dealing with the situation.

3. List the **D**isadvantages and **A**dvantages of each option.

4. Choose a **S**olution and follow through.

I went through the steps with Savannah, who already knew the problem – **how to respond to Mary's name-calling.** Then we thought of options to deal with it.

One option was to make fun of Mary's hair. Savannah thought posting bad things about Mary online was a good option, too.

I suggested Savannah do what we learned in school: *"When rumors fly, go directly to the person who made you cry."*

Then I told Savannah to list the disadvantages and advantages of each option.

	DISADVANTAGES	ADVANTAGES
TELL MARY HER HAIR IS A RAT'S NEST	- Mary fights back. - I get in trouble.	- I get even. - Mary feels as bad as I do.
POST SOMETHING BAD ABOUT MARY ONLINE	- I can't take it back. - Parents and teachers see it. - I'm a cyberbully.	- I feel better – at first. - No one will mess with me again.
ASK MARY DIRECTLY IF SHE SAID I WAS A MEANIE	- Have to talk face-to-face (might be uncomfortable). - Mary might call me a name again.	- Mary may apologize. - Mary says it was all a misunderstanding, and we save our friendship.

I told Savannah to think really hard about each option. Then she should pick the one that has the best chance of fixing the problem and making everyone happy.

She decided to speak directly to Mary.

Great choice! Right away, Mary admitted to calling her a meanie. She only said it because she was mad about not getting invited to **Savannah's BIG birthday BASH.**

"But I did invite you!" Savannah shouted.
"I put the invite in your locker."

Mary ran to her locker and looked inside. Sure enough, there it was. All crumpled in a messy stack.

"Sorry, Savannah," Mary said. "Guess I should have talked to you first instead of getting all mad. I promise not to do that again."

21

I told my teacher, Mrs. Green, that I felt like a professional problem solver after saving Savannah and Mary's friendship.

Mrs. Green told me she liked that strategy. Then she said, *"You know, Braden, SODAS aren't only for solving a negative problem. You can use this process to help make other decisions, too.* For example, what if you got invited to two parties at the same time? SODAS could help you decide what to do."

She's right!

I sooo wanted to use my **AWESOME problem-solving skills** again. But it wasn't until the day of the big kickball game that I had a problem to solve... **AND IT WAS A BIG ONE.**

My kickball team was seconds away from playing in the championship game. When the recess bell **FINALLY** rang, I jumped from my desk and sprinted towards the door. But just as I was about to go out and play, I heard the voice of Mrs. Green.

"But what about kickball?"

I pouted, and then dropped to the floor.

I sat against the wall wondering if I should sneak out.

Then a picture of my dad holding two SODA cans popped into my head. It was a sign I had to think of other options. Options that wouldn't get me into trouble, like finishing my homework really fast.

Sneak out?

Sit and pout?

Do my homework?

Those were my options, and each had advantages and disadvantages.

Homework
Assignment
LATE

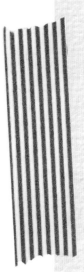

	DISADVANTAGES	ADVANTAGES
SNEAK OUT TO RECESS	- Makes Mrs. Green mad. - Get caught and I'll be in big trouble. - Still have to finish homework.	- Get to play kickball. - Being sneaky is exciting. - Don't have to do homework right now.
POUT AND DO NOTHING	- Miss recess. - Boring. - Homework doesn't get done.	- Everyone feels sorry for me. - Don't have to do homework right now.
FINISH MY HOMEWORK	- Miss part of recess. - Might not get to play. - No fun.	- May get SOME recess time. - Homework gets done. - I look responsible.

I decided to do the assignment super fast – and right – so I wouldn't have to do it over again.

It was the best thing to do, and I didn't want to get into any more trouble. I even finished before recess was over, but not in enough time to go outside – UGH.

At least I was a **winner at problem solving!**

When I got home, Dad had a surprise for Mom.

"Boys, I'm baking Mom's favorite cake and I think you're going to love it too."

"Uh... that's a **BIG NO** for me, Dad. I don't eat **ANYTHING** that's smoking."

Dad jumped up.

"NOoooooooooo!"

he yelled. *"I forgot to take the cake out of the oven.*

I'm not sure there's a way to solve THIS problem!"

Smiling, I walked into the kitchen holding two cans of soda, a pencil, and paper. Little did Dad know, **SODAS** were about to save his **surprise.**

The one thing all of us have in common is that we have to solve problems and challenges of various degrees and complexities.

A lucky few among us always seem to resolve complex problems successfully by thinking critically and logically. Still, even the most talented problem solvers need practice (and experience!) to develop and perfect this skill.

Here are a few tips you can use to help children learn how to become problem-solving pros!

1. Give kids the chance to come up with their own solutions. Sure, it's hard watching children struggle to solve a problem. But if you give them a chance to resolve an issue on their own, you encourage their independence and instill the confidence they need to solve future challenges.

2. Help children break down large problems into small, more manageable ones. Sometimes, kids get overwhelmed when a problem seems too big to handle. Help them look at problem situations as a series of small issues to be solved. The less anxious and emotional they are, the easier it becomes to think logically, patiently and methodically.

3. Allow for failure. Children need to understand that mistakes are fine as long as they learn from them. Treat mistakes as learning opportunities by asking kids to identify what went wrong and what could they have done differently to achieve a better outcome.

4. Share your problem-solving experiences. Talk to children about challenges you encountered and your response. Kids love hearing stories from their parents and teachers, and your insights can give them new tools to try when they face similar situations.

5. Seek a child's advice, when appropriate. Kids should never be burdened with "adult" problems, but asking them for help with a lighthearted situation provides many benefits. Kids gain valuable problem-solving experience, and they get a chance to look at things from another person's perspective, helping them learn empathy. It also can provide a sense of triumph when they solve a problem for someone else.

6. Make problems fun by posing hypothetical situations and asking kids how they would handle them. This encourages creative and critical thinking, and can reinforce the fact that there can be many different ways to solve problems successfully.

REMEMBER

Sometimes problems are just choices! And SODAS* work for those too!

For more parenting information, visit boystown.org/parenting.

SODAS* work!

* SODAS are part of the Boys Town Model®

Boys Town Press books by Bryan Smith

Kid-friendly books for teaching social skills

Executive FuNction

Downloadable Activities
Go to BoysTownPress.org
to download.

978-1-944882-11-2

978-1-944882-31-0

OTHER TITLES: What Were You Thinking? and *My Day Is Ruined!*

978-1-944882-20-4

978-1-944882-38-9

When I couldn't get Over it, I learned to Start Acting Differently
A story about managing SADness
Written by Bryan Smith

978-1-944882-22-8

Is There an App for That?
Written by Bryan Smith
Illustrated by Katie Wish
Hailey Discovers HAPPiness through Self-Acceptance

978-1-934490-74-7

Without Limits
dream • connect • soar

978-1-944882-36-5

978-1-944882-29-7

978-1-944882-12-9

978-1-944882-01-3

IF WINNING ISN'T EVERYTHING, WHY DO I HATE TO LOSE?
Written by BRYAN SMITH
Illustrated by BRIAN MARTIN

978-1-934490-85-3

BOYS TOWN Press

For information on Boys Town and its Education Model, Common Sense Parenting®, and training programs:
boystowntraining.org | boystown.org/parenting
training@BoysTown.org | 1-800-545-5771

For parenting and educational books and other resources:
BoysTownPress.org
btpress@BoysTown.org | 1-800-282-6657